The Lost Boy

A

CHAPEL HILL

BOOK

Illustrations by Ed Lindlof

The University of North Carolina Press

Chapel Hill & London

The Lost Boy

A Novella by Thomas Wolfe

Edited and with an Introduction by James W. Clark, Jr.

© 1992

The University of

North Carolina Press and

Paul Gitlin, Administrator, C.T.A.

Estate of Thomas Wolfe

Introduction by James W. Clark, Jr. © 1992

The University of North Carolina Press

Manufactured in the United States of America

96 95 94 93 92   5 4 3 2

Library of Congress Cataloging-in-Publication Data

Wolfe, Thomas, 1900–1938.

The lost boy : a novella / by Thomas Wolfe ;

edited and with an introduction by James W. Clark, Jr.

p.   cm.

"A Chapel Hill book."

ISBN 0-8078-2063-6 (cloth : alk. paper)

I. Clark, James William, 1943– .   II. Title.

PS3545.O337L7   1992   92-53704

813'.52—dc20

CIP

IN MEMORY OF

Richard Gaither Walser

Contents

A c k n o w l e d g m e n t s

In my search for the original text of *The Lost Boy*, I have enjoyed the indulgence of many people who were kindly disposed to this project. I am especially grateful to Mr. Paul Gitlin, Administrator, C.T.A. of the Estate of Thomas Wolfe. Several years ago he granted me access to certain Wolfe papers pertaining to and derived from *The Lost Boy* in the William E. Wisdom Collection of the Houghton Library at Harvard University. Now Mr. Gitlin has permitted me to publish this novella in special memory of Grover Wolfe, who was born in 1892, a century ago.

This splendid commemorative testimonial in the style and with the verve of Wolfe's typical fiction could not have become a centennial book without the additional assistance and support I have received from Suzanne Stutman, Aldo Magi, Charlene Turner, Joanne Mauldin, Terry Roberts, John and Sylvia Gordon, Ted Mitchell, Rodney Dennis, Christi Stanforth, and David Perry, my editor. I am also grateful to the College of Humanities and Social Sciences at North Carolina State University and to both the Thomas Wolfe Society and the North Caroliniana Society.

Introduction

In 1929 Thomas Wolfe made himself famous by portraying his voluble Asheville family as the memorable Gants of Altamont in *Look Homeward, Angel.* His proud and prescient mother always insisted, nonetheless, that an older son named Grover, not her youngest child Tom, was the brightest and best of her offspring. Born in 1900, Wolfe could barely remember this remarkable brother their mother continued to long for and memorialize; but he, too, craved information about Grover, as letters, notebook entries, an autobiographical outline, and two chapters of his first novel illustrate. In early March 1937 Wolfe completed a hauntingly beautiful and mysterious account of his own search for Grover. This belated addition to the Gant cycle of his fiction is the four-part novella entitled *The Lost Boy.*

In each part of this work Wolfe presents Grover from the perspective of a different family member. Part I is a third-person prose poem that relates Grover's own impressions and comprehensions of his afternoon experiences on the hometown square in April 1904. The father defends Grover in an episode that leaves the quiet boy changed forever. Part II presents Grover through his mother's adoring eyes; she focuses especially on a long-ago train trip that same April to St. Louis and the World's Fair. An older sister gives her acutely personal retrospection from the 1930s in Part III. In Part IV the youngest brother relates his own unsuccessful attempt to find Grover in the hot darkness of a late summer evening as he returns to the house in St. Louis where the family had spent seven months more than thirty years earlier.

Wolfe wrote *The Lost Boy* during a very demanding period, a time when he was realizing and expressing an expansion of his already abundant curiosities and human sympathies. Assisted by his splendid agent Elizabeth Nowell, he produced short novels like this one. He was also setting his giant compass on his southern mountain home for the first time since he had become famous. Moreover, Wolfe was anxious about his health and finances. As soon as the novella about Grover Gant was finished, Nowell helped Wolfe edit a short story out of it, and *Redbook Magazine* soon paid him $1,500 for this version — the largest sum he had ever received for a story. With some of this income he paid his passage from New York to Asheville later in the spring of 1937 when he went to visit his mother at home for the first time since the publication of *Look Homeward, Angel*. During the summer he returned for a longer, working vacation. That November "The Lost Boy" appeared in *Redbook* with the title character renamed Robert.

In September 1938 Elizabeth Nowell was in Baltimore with Julia Wolfe and her daughter Mabel when Wolfe lay dying of tuberculosis of the brain at Johns Hopkins Hospital. According to Nowell's biography of the author, when Mrs. Wolfe was told by Dr. Walter Dandy that her famous son was doomed, she instantly reverted to her memories of Grover and expressed them almost exactly as Wolfe had in Part II of *The Lost Boy*: "Child, child, it was so long ago, but when I hear the name again, it all comes back, as if it happened yesterday. And the old raw sore is open. I can see him just the way he was, the way he looked. . . ."

Edward Aswell of Harper and Brothers, the last editor to work personally with Wolfe, included a short version of *The Lost Boy* — different from the *Redbook* text — in the 1941 posthumous collection called *The Hills Beyond*. It is this rendition of the story based on Grover Wolfe that has become critically acclaimed, while the 1937 story that Wolfe and Nowell cut out of the novella and sold remains less well known. It is true that Francis E. Skipp selected the *Redbook* version for his 1987 edition of *The Complete Short Stories of Thomas Wolfe*. Yet by doing so he effectively moved the work out of the Gant cycle in which the novella is written, for he retained *Robert* as the name for Grover Gant.

By the time Wolfe wrote *The Lost Boy*, he had, in fact, largely moved from his Gant cycle to his Webber cycle, with George Webber succeeding Eugene Gant as the semi-autobiographical protagonist of his fictional world. In the 1939 posthumous novel *The Web and the Rock*, George Webber comments on the changes in the life of a boy between his twelfth and thirteenth years by entitling his own inaugural story "The End of the Golden Weather." This title is especially instructive for readers of Part I of *The Lost Boy*. Grover's father powerfully defends his son, but Mr. Gant cannot restore the boy's lively dream of life, his shimmering lights of boyhood. In the words of chapter 15 of *The Web and the Rock*, "For the first time, some of the troubling weathers of a man's soul are revealed to him . . . for the first time, he becomes aware of the thousand changing visages of time; and how his clear and radiant legend of the earth is, for the first time, touched with confusion and bewilderment, menaced by terrible depths and enigmas of experience he has never known before." George Webber's story opens with a twelve-year-old boy in his uncle's front yard at three o'clock in the afternoon. *The Lost Boy* opens as Grover, about that age, comes into the three o'clock radiance of the square, that haggis of images of abundance and loss, of fixity and change.

From Wolfe family photographs we know that Julia Wolfe and her son Grover looked remarkably alike. He is more than her physical tally, however. The mother's account of her lost boy in the second part of the novella presents him as an ace trader like herself, complete with her coloring, her hair. He also has her strong racial prejudices and pride. In the father's absence on the trip to St. Louis, young Grover is the man of the Gant family. It is he who tells their black retainer Simpson Featherstone to leave their train car and return to his accustomed place – although the Jim Crow laws in force back home are not the code of Indiana. Confronted by Grover, the black man obeys; years later the boy's proud mother still exults.

In bringing this particular family episode to light in *The Lost Boy*, Wolfe's fiction shows the extent to which his brother Grover had been, would always be, the best and brightest Wolfe child in their mother's judgment. Grover is her double, body and soul. That this illustrative Jim Crow episode is among the numerous cuts made in the narrative as Wolfe and Nowell shaped it for a magazine audience is especially regrettable. The honest passage, however troubling to modern readers, is one more indication of what the famous son believed his mother's immense pride in Grover amounted to. Elizabeth Nowell, for her part, understood what Wolfe intended by the full novella portrait he had originally provided of this mother-son team. In a March 5, 1937 letter, included by Richard S. Kennedy in *Beyond Love and Loyalty*, the agent wrote to the author that she had cut his edited typescript down to magazine size and popular taste in desperation. She knew, she said, that some of her suggested excisions would probably make Wolfe's heart bleed.

Grover's inventory of Garrett's grocery store on the square in Part I is another example of significant material left out of the *Redbook* version. So is the description in Part IV of Eugene's dark evening of hot despair in St. Louis. The one balances the other by contrasting kinds and tones of perceived abundance or excess. Neither these instances at the opening and closing of this short novel nor Grover's bold confrontation of Simpson Featherstone on the train in Part II has been known or even expected by readers of Wolfe until now.

Wolfe's artistic power in the short novel form is neither unknown nor unexpected, however. Both C. Hugh Holman and David Herbert Donald have stressed the effective demonstration of Wolfe's literary genius in the novella. Donald comments in *Look Homeward: A Life of Thomas Wolfe* that even if Wolfe himself had demurred, "little books would have been good for Wolfe's reputation. They would have demonstrated that, whatever Wolfe's limitations in crafting a long novel, he displayed a splendid sense of artistry in the short novel of 15,000 to 40,000 words. . . . Years later C. Hugh Holman edited five of *The Short Novels of Thomas*

Wolfe, which reminded readers that this was the form in which Wolfe worked best."

The Lost Boy is not included in Holman's 1961 collection, nor is it incorporated into one of the novels that Wolfe considered real writing. But this novella is a finely crafted realization of the author's genius for little books, especially this one he had contemplated so long and so actively. If Wolfe could not find Grover — even by visiting the house in St. Louis in 1935 — his concentrated sense of artistry has found in this four-part tribute a most memorable way to express the spacious presence of his, and our, abundant sense of loss. Here is more of Wolfe's magic in a dusty world.

Readers inspired to look further for information about what happened to Grover Wolfe will be rewarded by examining chapters 17 and 18 of *Thomas Wolfe and His Family* (1961) by Mabel Wolfe Wheaton and LeGette Blythe. Julia Wolfe left us no independent account of her favorite child. The final chapter of *The Marble Man's Wife* by Hayden Norwood is the closest nonfictional approximation of her views.

James W. Clark, Jr.

Part I

. . . . Light came and went and came again, the booming strokes of three o'clock beat out across the town in thronging bronze, light winds of April blew the fountain out in rainbow sheets, until the plume returned and pulsed, as Grover turned into the Square. He was a child dark-eyed and grave, birthmarked upon his neck — a berry of warm brown — and with a gentle face, too quiet, and too listening for his years. The scuffed boys' shoes, the thick-ribbed stockings gartered at the knees, the short knee pants cut straight with three small useless buttons at the side, the sailor blouse, the old cap battered out of shape, perched sideways up on top the raven head, the old soiled canvas bag slung from the shoulder, empty now, but waiting for the crisp sheets of the afternoon — these friendly shabby garments, shaped by Grover, uttered him. He turned and passed along the north side of the square and in that moment saw the union of forever and of now.

Light came and went and came again, the great plume of the fountain pulsed and winds of April sheeted it across the square, in rainbow gossamer of spray. The fire department horses drummed on the floors with wooden stomp, most casually, and with dry whiskings of their clean coarse tails. The street cars ground into the square from every portion of the compass and halted briefly like wound toys in their old familiar quarter-hourly formula of assembled Eight. And a dray, hauled by a boneyard nag, rattled across the cobbles on the other side before his father's shop. The court house bell boomed out its solemn warning of immediate three, and everything was just the same as it had always been.

He saw that haggis of vexed shapes with quiet eyes — that shabby accident of brick and stone, that hodgepodge of ill-sorted architectures that made up the square and he did not feel lost. For "Here," Grover thought, "here is the square as it has always been — and papa's shop, the fire department and the city hall, the fountain, pulsing with its plume, the light that comes and goes and comes again, the old dray rattling past, the boneyard nag, the street cars coming in and halting at the quarter hour, the hardware store on the corner there, and next to it, the library with a tower and battlements along the roof, as if it were an ancient castle, the row of old brick buildings on this side of the street, the people passing and the cars that come and go, the light that comes and changes and that always will come back again, and everything that comes and goes and changes in the square, and yet will be the same again – here," Grover thought, "here is the square that never changes, that will always be the same. Here is the month of April 1904. Here is the court house bell and three o'clock. And here is Grover with his paper bag. Here is old Grover, almost twelve years old – here is the square that never changes, here is Grover, here his father's shop, and here is time."

For so it seemed to him, small center of his little universe, itself the accidental masonry of twenty years, the chance agglomerate of time and of disrupted strivings. It was for him in his soul's picture the earth's pivot, the granite core of changelessness, the eternal place where all things came and passed and which abode forever and would never change.

He passed the old shack on the corner – the wooden firetrap where S. Goldberg ran his wiener stand – and then the Singer place next door, with its gleaming display of new machines, its fascinating calendar with the lay-out of the Singer works, – the tremendous buildings in exciting red, the grass plots of an unbelievable intensity of green, the lovely freight train with a locomotive like a model toy, curving in out of the toy perfection of the countryside, the huge water tower, itself as perfect as a toy, and the green grass all around. And before the factory there were fountains playing, and splendid boulevards crowded with a glittering traffic of fine carriages, proud Victorias drawn by prancing horses with arched necks, driven by coachmen with high hats, and bearing lovely ladies holding parasols.

It was a lovely place, and it always made him happy just to look at it. It was New Jersey, Pennsylvania or New York. It was a place that he had never seen, but the grass grew greener there, the brick was redder, the freight train and the water tower, the proud prancing horses, the splendid symmetry of everything, including nature, beat anything that he had ever seen and gave him a good feeling. It was The North, The North, the shining and enchanted North, the North of the green grass, the red barn and the perfect houses, the pleasant and symmetric North, where even the freight trains and the engines always wore a bright new coat of paint. It was the North, where even factory hands wore crisp blue overalls as tidy as a soldier's uniform, where even the rivers were a sapphire blue, and where there were no rough edges anywhere. It was the North, the perfect, shining, happy and symmetric North. It was the North, his father's land, where some day he would go. He paused a moment, looking through the window; that lavish and well painted landscape filled him as it always did with a sense of comfort and expectancy.

He saw the bright perfection of the sewing machines as well. He saw them and admired them, but he felt no joy.

They depressed him. They brought back to him the busy hum of housework and of women sewing, the intricacy of stitch and weave, the mystery of style and pattern, the memory of women bending over flashing needles, the pedalled tread, the busy whir. He knew there was some mystery in it that he could never fathom. The women took some joy in it that he could never understand. It was women's work: it filled him with unknown associations of dullness and of vague depression. And always, also, with a moment's twinge of horror, for his dark eye would always travel towards that flashing needle, that needle stitching up and down so fast the eye could never follow it. And then he would remember how his mother once had told him she had driven the needle through her finger, and always, when he passed this place, he would remember it and for a moment crane his neck and turn his head away.

Inside the shop he could see Mr. Thrash, the manager. And Mr. Thrash was tall and gaunt and sinewy. He had sandy hair, a sandy mustache, and big horse-like teeth. He had strong muscles in his jaws and they worked constantly. And when they worked, his horse-like teeth were bared in quick grimace. Mr. Thrash was strung on nervous wires and all his movements were quick and nervous, and his voice was quick and nervous too. And yet he knew that Mr. Thrash was good. He liked Mr. Thrash. There was something good and quick and strong and sandy in him.

He saw Grover now and bared his big horse teeth for just a fraction of a second, and waved his sandy-knuckled hand at him and turned away, just as if he had been strung on wires. And Grover always wondered how Mr. Thrash had got into this woman's business. Then he would see the splendid picture of the Singer factory and think of it and Mr. Thrash together. And then he would feel good again.

He passed on then, but had to stop again next door before the music store. He always had to stop by places that had shining perfect things in them. He loved hardware stores and windows full of accurate geometric tools. He loved windows full of hammers, saws and planing boards. He liked windows full of strong new rakes and hoes, with unworn handles, of white perfect wood, stamped hard and vivid with the maker's seal. He liked a tool box full of brand new tools. He loved to see such things as these in the windows of the hardware stores. And he would fairly gloat upon them and think that some day he would own a set himself.

He liked places with good smells in them. He liked to look at livery stables and to see what was going on inside. He liked the thick-planked floors of livery stables, all dented, pulped and shredded by the horses' hoofs. He liked to watch the niggers with the horses, to see the niggers groom the horses with a currycomb, to see the niggers slap the horses on their shining rumps and growl in nigger horse-talk – "Whoa – git over dar!" He liked to see the niggers take the harness off and walk the horse out of the buggy shafts. He liked the way the horse walked on the wooden floor – a kind of stately and stiff-jointed walk. And he liked the casual way the horse would lift its proud coarse tail and let fall an oaty dropping. He liked the look of all these things on livery stable floors.

He liked the little offices at the side of livery stables also. He liked these dingy little offices with their grimy windows, their little cast-iron stoves, their planked floors, their battered little safe, their creaky chairs with barrel backs, their smells of horse and harness and of sweat-cured leather and their company of livery stable men, florid, fresh-complexioned, leather-legginged, coarse-tongued, full of sudden bursts of fat strong laughter. He liked such things as these.

He didn't like the look of banks, of real estate or fire insurance offices, he liked drug stores and the pungent, clean nostalgic smells of them, he liked drug store windows with great jars of colored water and with white balls going up and down. He did not like windows full of patent medicines and hot water bags, for somehow they depressed him. He liked barber shops, tobacco shops, but he did not like the windows of an undertaker's place. He did not like the roll-top desk nor the diploma that hung over it, nor the potted plant, nor the drooping fern. He did not like the dark look of the place behind it. He didn't like an undertaker's shop and therefore he would never stop before it.

He didn't like the look of coffins either, although they were elegant and grand. And yet, he liked pianos, even though a piano always made him think a little of a coffin. He didn't like the way a coffin smelled and yet somehow he liked the way a big piano smelled. It made him think of home and of the closed and slightly stale smell of the parlor, which he liked. It reminded him of the parlor and the parlor carpet, which was thick and brown and faded, and which was always swept most carefully every morning. It made him think of the glass chandelier, with all the little shining pendants of cut-glass, and the way they flashed and clashed when some one touched them.

It made him think of the wax fruit on the parlor mantel, with the glass covering over it, and of the music rack of old dark wood, and of the table, with its slab of streaky marble, which his father had carved himself, and of the enormous Bible, so big and cumbersome he could hardly lift it, and of the great fat album with the metal clasps, the daguerreo-types of his father as a boy, all of the brothers, sisters, and the other people, touched faintly on the cheeks with dabs of pink.

It made him think of the stereoscope, and all the pic-tures that he never tired of looking at, of being there alone on quiet afternoons and looking unweariedly through the stereoscope at all the pictures of Gettysburg, of Seminary Ridge and Devil's Den, spread thick with sprawled out forms in gray and blue.

And finally it made him think of the big piano in the par-lor, the great shining sweep and spread of it, its coffin-like magnificence, and its rich and goodly smell. It made him think of how, before he got too big for childish things like that, he loved to crawl beneath the great piano and just sit there on the carpet, smelling it all in, and thinking, feeling, getting from it all a sense of thrilling solitude, of isolation and of proud possession, a kind of strange dark comfort — he did not know why.

Therefore, he always stopped before the music and piano store. It was a splendid store. And in the window was a small white dog upon his haunches, with head cocked gravely to one side, a small white dog that never moved, that never barked, that listened attentively at the flaring funnel of a horn to hear 'His Master's Voice' – a horn forever silent, and a voice that never spoke. And within, were many rich and shining shapes of great pianos, an air of splendor and of wealth. And to one side, a counter, behind which Mr. Markham stood.

He liked Mr. Markham too. He was a small brisk man, and everything about him was very brisk and clean. He had a small brisk mustache of cropped gray. His hair was graying too, and he let it grow out thick, abundant. But somehow, even his hair had a cropped brisk look, as if every separate hair were standing cleanly, briskly, forth. And Mr. Markham's face, his features, were also small and clean and brisk, and very delicate. He was a Yankee, and he had the Yankee way of talking – everything crisp and clear and brisk and full of clean decision – and when he waited on some one, he would stand behind the counter with his fingers arched upon the counter and his head cocked briskly, sidewise, while he listened to the customer's request. Then, when he had heard all the customer had to say, he would nod quickly, briskly, in his bird-like way, and say, professionally, "Uh-huh!," very much the way a dentist says it when he is telling you that you can spit, and then go quickly, briskly, on his errand to get the piece of music that the customer had asked for.

He never seemed to be in doubt about anything. If he had the piece of music, he knew instantly that he had it, and he knew exactly where to find it. And he would go quickly, briskly, instantly, to the exact place where the music was.

And if he did not have the music, he would shake his head in the same quick manner, with a pleasant smile, touched crisply with regret, and say, "I'm sorry, but it's not in stock." Everything Mr. Markham did was like that – clean and brisk and certain. He was a funny little man. But he pleased and tickled Grover. Grover liked him. He liked to stop and look at him, to see him with his fingers arched, his head turned bird-like, listening.

Next door was Garrett's grocery store and Grover had to stop here too. It was a fine place, a fine wide store that ran the whole way through back to the other street, and full of pleasant smells. The big sweet pickle barrel was to the left and farther down there was an even bigger barrel for the dill pickles. And on the counter to the right there was always a yellow, round, enormous cheese, with a great V-shaped wedge cut cleanly from it. And beside this was the coffee grinder, and beside the coffee grinder were the scales. And behind the counter were great bins for coffee, grits and rice, great bins that pulled out scoop-wise. And on both sides, up to the ceilings, were the loaded shelves, shelves crowded with a staggering abundance of things, with jellies and preserves, with bottled relish and with pickles, with ketchup, sardines and canned salmon, with canned tomatoes, corn and peas, and pork and beans. And everything that one could ever want, and more than one had ever tasted, more than one could ever think of, or consume. Enough, thought Grover, for a city. Enough, it seemed to him, to feed every one in town.

And in the back there was a great pile of sacked flour, and great slabs of fatback, racked up like cord wood.

And behind all this there were some tall gaunt windows, not very clean, and guarded with iron bars. The windows made him think of the back of an American store, the blank plane of cakey brick, the loading platform, just the way that things have always looked here in America – the kind of buildings we have always had – all of it somehow like the Civil War, and Sherman's troopers entering Atlanta, some boxcars on the tracks, a little of the depot and the engine with funnel spout and the soldiers coming up past buildings like this of old cakey brick, stark plain, a sign that says 'J. Wilson, Printer's Shop' – or 'Grocer' – and behind the old gaunt windows barred, the loading platform and red clay. It always made the boy a little desolate, and a little happy. It was perhaps a question of the season and the light. For light would come and go — when light was right then even cakey brick and blankness could be wonderful — it was too hard to utter — and a boy of less than twelve could not utter it. Just say it was America, it was the South; familiar as man's flesh and blood — familiar as raw winds in March — as a raw throat or a running nose — red mirey clay and desolation — or April, April, and wild loveliness — just say that it was all this — raw, cakey, desolate, lovely, lyrical, and full of wonder — just say that it was hard to utter — America, old cakey brick, a grocer's shop, and April — and the South.

And over all and into all and through all, permeating everything until it seemed to have soaked into the very wood upon the counter, until it seemed to have been worn in, and seasoned the very planks upon the floor, one single, multiple, complex, all-inclusive, indefinable but glorious All-Smell — a smell not to be spoken of, because there were no words for it, a smell that could not be described because there was no language for it, a smell that never could be named, because there was no name for it. All you could say was, there was in it a smell of firm and pungent yellow cheese, the smell of the sweet pickle barrel and the smell of dill, the smell of fresh ground coffee and of tea, the smell of bacon fatback and of country ham, the smell of country butter and of milk, the smell of all good things and succulent that ever yet had been, each in itself, alone and separate, altogether mixed and mingled, blended, in a maddening aroma, this great All-Smell, for which there was no name.

For there was not only in these smells the recognition of remembered things, the knowledge of their separate identities. There was more, far more, than this — so much of magic of association, of impossible desire. There was in them, he knew not how — he only knew that it was there — the smell of India and Brazil, the smell of the dark South and of the golden and unknown West, the smell of the great and splendid North, the smell of England and of France, of mighty rivers and of great plantations, of unknown peoples and strange tongues, all the glory of the world unknown, all the splendor of the world unvisited, all the mystery, the beauty, the magnificence of the mighty earth, as it was built in shining images in the proud and flaming vision of a child.

He had to stop and look a moment now, he could not pass. It was like going by Arabia. Before the store stood the horse and the delivery wagon, the old gray horse, drooped gauntly to his hitching weight. From time to time the old horse lifted its gaunt hind quarter and dug sharply at the street. He knew the old horse well, he always saw it with a pleasant memory — a memory of summer and of sudden rain. He had been coming through the square on such a day. It had been hot. The clouds had gathered suddenly. They had *collected*, really, with a sulphurous and electric threat. And now, the whole air brooded with the threat of storm. The light went violet, the cloud collected to its thunder tip. And suddenly the lightning broke, the storm crashed down.

It came at once and in torrential deluge, such as he had never seen. It just crashed down on them, as if the Mississippi had burst from the sky. It just fell instantly and heavily. And in a moment the whole square was bare of life as if it were the ruin of an ancient city. The rain hissed down, the gutters foamed with water, the sidewalks ran like open sluices, the gutter spouts belched out a tumbling flood. And Grover ducked for cover in the grocery store. He looked out on that torrential deluge, on that barren square. He heard the great storm crash, and he felt joy.

Nothing now was left upon the square except the grocery wagon and the old gray horse. Storm hit the wagon, swept sheet-wise cross the roof. The rain came down in torrents on the horse, the old horse bent its head. The rain tore down and smote upon its flanks. It hissed and spouted off the long ridge of its bony back. It smoked off its gaunt old ribs, spouted into the sockets of its bony hips. The old horse kept its head down patiently, and the flood descended. It howled and tore across the square in blinding sheets. It ripped and tore at awnings, it came down like an avalanche that drove and hurled against the buildings, till the whole square was a sheet of water.

And suddenly, almost as quick as it had come, the storm was over. The inky darkness swept away, light broke into the square again, the gulleys and the gutters hissed and gurgled running water. And the old horse stood there, reeking wet, and somehow with a look of tired gratefulness, and lifted its old head, its long gray neck, and, in a moment, shifted stiffly, dug its hoof upon the street.

And Grover stood there watching, saw it all. It filled him, somehow, with a sense of wonder, magic, and of happiness. And he could not forget the inky and sulphuric skies, cloud-crested with electric pregnancy, the dark and brooding sinister of light, a kind of numb and pending ecstasy in his entrails as he waited.

And then the glorious crashing of the storm, the howling

and torrential fury of it. And the old horse bent against the storm, like an old rock of time. And he could not forget; whenever after that, he would see the old gray horse or think of it, he would remember time, the magic light, the magic coming of the storm on that lost summer's day, the wild and savage joy of it, and all the smells, the darkness and the people waiting in the grocery store.

And now he saw the horse again and thought of it and looked into the store with the kind of deep and nameless rapture that the store always gave to him. He breathed deep of it, and drunk its glorious and pervasive smell into his lungs. He looked at it with longing, with delight, and with mysterious wonder, with humor and affection too. He did not know the reason, but the people in the store, Mr. Garrett and the grocery clerks, always roused in him this kind of humor and affection. It was the unction of them, maybe — a kind of oily unction when they spoke to customers, a kind of lisping unction in their tones, as if butter wouldn't melt upon their tongues. They were so suave, so oily, so persuasive as they talked.

Even as he looked, the phone rang and Mr. Garrett went to take the order. He took the receiver from the hook, the pencil from his ear, it was a single practiced movement. He began to write the order on a pad. He was a man in his mid-forties, with neat wings of hair exactly parted in the middle. And somehow, this always tickled Grover — it seemed so appropriate. He wore a long white apron, and he had straw cuffs about his forearms. The wrinkles of his shallow forehead arched coyly as he spoke across the phone, — and oh but butter wouldn't melt on Mr. Garrett's tongue, the way he talked. "Yes ma'am, yes ma'am . . . Oh yes, indeed, Mrs. Jarvis . . . *Yes*, indeed. Oh they're very nice. Very nice, indeed. . . . Yes, ma'am. We just got them in this morning. . . . Yes ma'am. Two dozen eggs . . . Two pounds of butter. Yes ma'am, oh it's very nice. One half dozen canned tomatoes. . . . Yes ma'am, yes ma'am. Oh, the very best. . . . Oh yes, indeed. We carry nothing but the highest grade. One pound of breakfast bacon. Yes ma'am." . . . Then with unctuous persuasiveness, very softly, "And coffee. . . . How are you off for coffee, Mrs. Jarvis? . . . We have a special sale this week, a special blend; it's two cents cheaper than the other, but I can recommend it to you highly. . . ." And so it went, until he ran through the whole stock, unctuously persuasive, fawningly obedient to do the lady's command, simply delighted about everything, as if butter wouldn't melt upon his tongue, until it fairly made your mouth water just to hear him talk of coffee, butter, or a pound of bacon.

"Old butter-lips," thought Grover, and for a moment a faint grin touched his quiet face. "Yes, we have some nice tomatoes — and we have some nice fresh potatoes — and we have some nice fresh onions — and how'd you like some nice fresh roas'n-ears, and some nice fresh corn on the cob, and some nice fresh? — some nice fresh? — " he reflected — "Oh, yes marm — some nice fresh Everything-There-Is!" Then he passed on.

And now, indeed, he *was* caught, held, suspended. A waft of air, warm, chocolate-laden, filled his nostrils. He tried to pass the white front of the little eight-foot shop, he paused, struggling with conscience, he could not go on. It was the little candy shop, run by old Crocker and his wife. And Grover could not pass.

"Old stingy Crockers!" he thought scornfully, "I'll not go there any more. They are so stingy they stop the clocks at night. But — " The maddening warmth and fragrance of rich cooking chocolate touched him once again. "I'll just look in the window and see what they've got." He paused a moment, looking with his dark and quiet eyes into the window of the little candy shop. The window cleanly papered, spotless clean, was filled with trays of fresh-made candy. His eyes rested for a moment on a tray of chocolate drops. Unconsciously he licked his lips. Put one of them upon your tongue and it just melted there, like honeydew. And then the trays full of rich home-made fudge. He gazed longingly at the deep body of the chocolate fudge, reflectively at maple walnut, more critically, yet with longing, at the mints, the nougatines, and all the other dainties.

"Old stingy Crockers!" Grover muttered once again, and turned to go. "I wouldn't go in *there* again."

And yet — and yet — he did not go away. "Old stingy Crockers," it was true; still, they did make the best candy in town, the best, in fact, that he had ever tasted.

He looked through the window back into the little shop and saw Mrs. Crocker there. A customer had gone in and had made a purchase and as Grover looked he saw Mrs. Crocker, with her little wrenny hands, her little wrenny face, her prim lips, her pinched features, lean over and peer primly at the scales. She had a piece of candy in her clean, bony, little fingers — it was, as Grover noted, a piece of walnut maple fudge. And as he looked, she broke it, primly, in her little bony hands. She dropped a morsel down into the scales. They weighted down alarmingly, and her thin lips tightened. She snatched a piece of fudge out of the scales with bony fingers and, peering primly, broke it carefully once again. This time the scale wavered, went down very slowly and came back again. Mrs. Crocker carefully put the reclaimed piece of fudge back in the tray, put the remainder in a paper bag, folded it and gave it to the customer, counted the money carefully and doled it out into the till, the pennies in one place, the nickels in another.

Grover stood there, looking scornfully. "Old stingy Crocker — afraid that she might give a crumb away."

He grunted scornfully and again he turned to go. But now another fact caught his attention. Just as he turned to go, Mr. Crocker came out from the little place behind the little partitioned place where they made all their candy, bearing a tray of fresh-made candy in his skinny hands. Old man Crocker rocked along the counter to the front and put it down. He really rocked along. He was a cripple. And like his wife, he was a wrenny, wizened little creature, with thin lips, a pinched and meager face. One leg was inches shorter than another, and on this leg there was an enormous thick soled boot, and to this boot there was attached a kind of wooden, rocker-like arrangement, six inches high at least, to make up for the deficiency of his game right leg. And on this wooden cradle Mr. Crocker rocked along. That was the only way you could describe it. A little, pinched and skinny figure of a man with bony hands and meager features, and when he walked he really rocked along, with a kind of prim and apprehensive little smile, as if he was afraid he was going to lose something.

"Old stingy Crocker," muttered Grover. "Humph! he wouldn't give you anything, would he?"

And yet he did not go away. He hung there curiously, peering through the window, with his dark and quiet eyes, with his dark and gentle face now focussed and intent, alert and curious, flattening his nose against the glass. Unconsciously he scratched the thick-ribbed fabric of one stockinged leg with the scruffed and worn toe of his old shoe. The fresh warm odor of the new-made fudge had reached him. It was delicious. It was a little maddening. Half consciously, still looking through the window with his nose pressed to the glass, he began to fumble in one trouser pocket and pulled out his purse, a shabby worn old black one with a twisted clasp. He opened it and prowled about inside.

What he found was not inspiring — a nickel and two pennies and — he had forgotten them! — the stamps. He took the stamps out and unfolded them. There were five twos, eight ones, all that remained of the dollar-sixty-cents worth which Reed, the pharmacist, had given him for running errands a week or two before.

"Old Crocker," Grover thought, and looked somberly at the grotesque little form as it rocked back into the shop again, around the counter, and up the other side.

"Well — " again he looked indefinitely at the stamps in his hand — "He's had all the rest of them. He might as well take these."

So, soothing conscience with this sop of scorn, he

opened the door and went into the shop and stood a moment looking at the trays in the glass case and finally decided. Pointing with slightly grimy finger at the fresh-made tray of chocolate fudge, he said, "I'll take fifteen cents worth of this, Mr. Crocker."

He paused a moment, fighting with embarrassment, then he lifted his dark face and said quietly, "And please, I'll have to give you stamps again."

Mr. Crocker made no answer. He did not look at Grover. He pressed his lips together primly. He went rocking away and got the candy scoop, came back, slid open the door of the glass case, put fudge into the scoop and, rocking to the scales, began to weigh the candy out. Grover watched him quietly. He watched him as he peered and squinted, he watched him purse and press his lips together, he saw him take a piece of fudge and break it in two parts. And then old Crocker broke two parts in two. He weighed, he squinted and he hovered, until it seemed to Grover that by calling *Mrs.* Crocker stingy he had been guilty of a rank injustice. Compared to her frugal mate, the boy reflected, she was a very cornucopia of abundance, a goddess of rich plenty. But finally, to his vast relief, the job was over, the scales hung there suspended, quivering apprehensively, upon the very hair-line of nervous balance, as if even the scales were afraid that one more move from Old Man Crocker and the scales would be undone.

Mr. Crocker took the candy then and dumped it in a paper bag and, rocking back along the counter towards the boy, he dryly said: "Where are the stamps?" Grover gave them to him. Mr. Crocker relinquished his claw-like hold upon the bag and set it down upon the counter. Grover took the bag and dropped it in his canvas sack, and then remembered. "Mr. Crocker — " again he felt the old embarrassment that was almost like strong pain — "I gave you too much," Grover said. "There were eighteen cents in stamps. — You — you can just give me three ones back."

Mr. Crocker did not answer for a moment. He was busy with his bony little hands, unfolding the stamps and flattening them out on top of the glass counter. When he had done so, he peered at them sharply, harshly, for a moment, thrusting his scrawny neck forward and running his eye up and down, as a bookkeeper who totes up rows of figures.

When he had finished, he did not look at Grover. He said tartly: "I don't like this kind of business. If you want candy, you should have the money for it. I'm not in the stamp business. I'm not the post office. I don't like this kind of business. The next time you come in here and want anything, you'll have to pay me money for it."

Hot anger rose in Grover's throat. His olive face suffused with angry color. His tarry eyes got black and bright. The hot words rose unbidden to his lips. For a moment he was on the verge of saying: "Then why did you take my other stamps? Why do you tell me now, when you have taken all the stamps I had, that you don't want them?"

But he was a boy, a boy of eleven years, a quiet, gentle, gravely thoughtful boy, and he had learned good manners, he had been taught how to respect his elders. So he just stood there looking with his tar-black eyes. Old Man Crocker, prim-lipped, pursing at the mouth a little, without meeting Grover's gaze, took the stamps up in his thin, parched fingers and, turning, rocked away with them down to the till.

He took the twos and folded them and laid them in one rounded scallop, then took the ones and folded them and put them in the one next to it. Then he closed the till and started to rock off, down towards the other end. Grover, his face now quiet and grave, kept looking at him, but Mr. Crocker did not look at Grover. Instead he began to take some [stamped] cardboard [shapes] and fold them into boxes.

In a moment Grover said, "Mr. Crocker, will you give me the three ones, please?"

Mr. Crocker did not answer. He kept folding boxes, he compressed his thin lips quickly as he did so. But Mrs. Crocker, back turned to her spouse, also folding boxes with her parsley hands, muttered tartly: "Hm! *I'd* give him nothing!"

Mr. Crocker looked up, looked at Grover, said, "What are you waiting for?"

"Will you give me the three ones, please?" Grover said.

"I'll give you nothing," Mr. Crocker said.

He left his work and came rocking forward along the counter. "Now you get out of here! Don't you come in here with any more of those stamps — " said Mr. Crocker.

"I should like to know where he gets them — that's what *I* should like to know," said Mrs. Crocker.

She did not look up as she said these words. She inclined her head, a little to the side, in Mr. Crocker's direction, and she continued to fold the boxes with her parsley fingers.

"You get out of here," said Mr. Crocker, "and don't you

come back here with any stamps. . . . Where did you get those stamps?" he said.

"That's just what *I've* been thinking," Mrs. Crocker said. "*I've* been thinking all along."

"You've been coming in here for the last two weeks with those stamps," said Mr. Crocker, "I don't like the look of it. Where did you get those stamps?" he said.

"That's what *I've* been thinking," said Mrs. Crocker, for a second time.

Grover had got white underneath his olive skin. His eyes had lost their luster. They looked like dull, stunned balls of tar. "From Mr. Reed," he said — "I got the stamps from Mr. Reed," said Grover. He burst out desperately, "Mr. Crocker, — Mr. Reed will tell you how I got the stamps. You ask Mr. Reed. I did some work for Mr. Reed, he gave me those stamps two weeks ago."

"Mr. Reed," said Mrs. Crocker acidly. She did not turn her head. "I call it mighty funny," Mrs. Crocker said.

"Mr. Crocker," Grover said, "if you'll just let me have three ones — "

"You get out of here," cried Mr. Crocker, and he began rocking forward towards Grover. "Now don't you come in here again, boy! There's something funny about this whole business! I don't like the look of it. I don't want your trade," said Mr. Crocker, "if you can't pay as other people do, then I don't want your trade."

"Mr. Crocker," Grover said again, and underneath the olive skin his face was gray, "if you'll just let me have those three — "

"You get out of here," Mr. Crocker cried, and began to

rock down towards the counter's end. "If you don't get out, boy – "

"*I'd* call a policeman, that's what *I'd* do," Mrs. Crocker said.

Mr. Crocker rocked around the lower end of the counter. He came rocking up towards Grover. "You get out," he said.

He took the boy and pushed him with his bony little hands, and Grover was sick and gray down to the hollow pit of his stomach.

"You've got to give me those three ones," he said.

"You get out of here!" shrilled Mr. Crocker. He seized the screen door, pulled it open, and pushed Grover out. "Don't you come back in here," he said, pausing for a moment, working thinly at the lips. He turned and rocked back in the shop again. The screen door slammed behind him. Grover stood there on the pavement. And light came and went and came again into the square.

The boy stood there a moment, and a wagon rattled past. There were some people passing by. The driver of the Garrett wagon came out with grocery-laden box and put it in the wagon and slammed up the lid. But Grover did not notice them, and later he could not remember them. He stood there blindly, gray beneath the olive, in the watches of the sun, feeling this was Time, this was the Square, this was the center of the universe, the granite core of changelessness, and feeling, this is Grover, this the Square, this is Now.

But something had gone out of day. He felt the overwhelming, the soul-sickening guilt that all the children, all the good men of the earth have felt since time began. And even anger had died down, had been drowned out, in this swelling and soul-sickening tide of guilt, and "This the Square" – thought Grover as before – "This is Now. There is my father's shop. And all of it is as it has always been – save I."

And the square reeled drunkenly around him, light went in blind gray motes before his eyes, the fountain sheeted out to rainbow iridescence and returned to its proud, pulsing plume again. But all the brightness had gone out of day, and "Here the Square, and here is permanence and here is time – and all of it the same as it has always been, save I."

The scuffed boots of the lost boy moved and stumbled blindly over. The numb feet crossed the pavement – reached the sidewalk, reached the plotted central square – the grass plots, and the flower beds, so soon with red and packed geraniums.

"I want to be alone," thought Grover, "where I can not go near him – oh God, I hope he never hears, that no one ever tells him – "

The plume blew out, the iridescent sheet of spray blew over him. He passed through, found the other side and crossed the street and – "Oh God, if papa ever hears," – thought Grover, as his numb feet started up the steps into his father's shop.

He found and felt the steps – the width and thickness of old lumber twenty feet in length – the draymen sprawled out on the other end, the whips long, snaking on the sidewalk, the square down-slanted to a funnel here, the cobbles, rude and strong, the side stairs going up into the calaboose; below, the market's arch of three o'clock, the slanting place for draymen and the country wagons, the dip and rise, the scarred and gullied clay of Niggertown, the shacks and houses, and beyond, the rim of hill, immensely near, just greening into April.

He saw it all – the iron columns on his father's porch, just shabby, painted with the dull anomalous black-green that all such columns in this land and weather come to; two angels, fly-specked, and the waiting stones; the fly-specked window of the jeweler, his window platform, his screwed eyeglass, and within, the little wooden fence around him, his great brow, his yellow wrinkled features, and a safe, great dust, much yellowed newspaper.

Beyond and all round, in the stonecutter's shop, cold shapes of white and marble, rounded stone, the base, the languid angel with strong marble hands of love.

The partition of his father's office was behind his shop. He went on down the aisle, the white shapes stood around him. He went on to the back of the workroom. This he knew – the little cast-iron stove in left-hand corner, caked, brown, heat-blistered, and the elbow of the long stack running out across the shop, the high, the dirty window, looking down across the market square towards Niggertown, the rude old shelves, plank-boarded, thick, the wood not smooth but pulpy, like the strong hair of an animal; upon the shelves the chisels of all sizes and a layer of stone dust; an emery wheel with pump tread, and a door that let out on the alleyway, yet the alleyway twelve feet below; a tin urinal, encrusted, copperous, stinking, and a wooden frame or screen of torn cotton that enclosed it. Here in the room, two trestles of this coarse spiked wood upon which rested gravestones, and at one, a man at work.

The boy looked, saw the name was Creasman: the carved analysis of John, the symmetry of S, the fine sentiment of Creasman, November — Nineteen — Three; — with much coarseness, much brown stubble, many pine trees, much red clay about and over him.

The man looked up. He was a man of fifty-three, gaunt-visaged, mustache cropped, immensely long and tall and gaunt. He must have been six feet and four, or more. He wore good clothes, good dark clothes — heavy, massive, — save he had no coat. He worked in shirt sleeves with his vest on, a strong watch chain stretching cross his vest, wing collar and black tie, Adam's apple, bony forehead, bony nose, light eyes, gray-green, undeep and cold, and, somehow, lonely-looking, a striped apron going up around his shoulder, and starched cuffs. And in his hand, the wooden mallet, not a hammer, but a tremendous rounded wooden mallet like a butcher's bole; and in his other hand, a strong cold chisel tool.

"How are you, son?"

He did not look up as he spoke. He spoke quietly, absently. He worked upon the chisel and the wooden mallet, as a jeweler might work on your watch, except that in the man and in the wooden mallet there was power too.

"What is it, son?" he said.

He moved around the table from the head, started up on J once again.

"Papa, I never stole the stamps," Grover said.

The man put down the mallet, laid the chisel down. He came around the trestle.

"What?" he said.

And Grover winked his tar-black eyes, they brightened, the hot tears shot out. "I never stole the stamps," he said.

"Hey? What is this?" the man said. "What stamps?"

"That Mr. Reed gave to me when the other boy was sick and I worked there for three days. And Old Man Crocker," Grover said, "he took all the stamps. And he took all the rest of them from me today. And I told him Mr. Reed had given them to me. And now he owes me three ones – and Old Man Crocker says he don't believe that they were mine – he says – I must have got them somewhere," Grover said.

"The stamps that Reed gave to you – hey?" the stonecutter said. "The stamps you had – " He wet his thumb upon his lips, he walked from his workshop out into the storeroom and cleared his throat and cried "Jannadeau – " But now Jannadeau, the jeweler, was not there.

The man came back, he cleared his throat, and as he passed the old gray painted board-partition of his office, he cleared his throat and wet his thumb, and said, "Now, I tell you – "

Then he turned and strode up towards the front again and, passing Jannadeau's little, fenced-in, grimy square, he cleared his throat and said, "I tell you now – " And coming back, along the aisle between the rows of marshalled gravestones, he said underneath his breath, "By God, now – "

He took Grover by the hand across the square. They went out flying. They went down along the aisle by all the gravestones, marble porch, the fly-specked angels waiting among the gravestones, the wooden steps, the draymen and the cobbled slant, the sidesteps of the calaboose, the city hall, the market, the four sides, not quite symmetric, of the square, the architectures and the brick, — across the whole thing, but they did not notice it.

And the fountain pulsed, the plume blew out in sheeted iridescence, and it swept across them, and an old gray horse, with torn lips, with a kind of peaceful look about his torn lips, swucked up the cool, the flowing and the mountain water from the trough as Grover and his father went across the square.

The man took the hand — the hand of his small son — the boy's hand was imprisoned, caught, in the stonecutter's hand and they strode down through the aisle, past the cold marbles, across the porch, where the two angels were, and down the steps, and by the draymen sitting on the step.

They went across the square through the sheeted iridescence of the spray and to the other side and to the candy shop. The man was dressed in his long apron still. He had not paused to change the long striped apron, he was still holding Grover by the hand. He opened the screen door and stepped inside. "Give him the stamps," he said. Mr. Crocker came rocking forward behind the counter, with the prim and careful look that now was somewhat like a smile. "It was just. . . ." he said.

"Give him the stamps," the man said, and threw some coins down on the counter.

Mr. Crocker rocked away and got the stamps. He came rocking back. "I just didn't know — " he said.

The stonecutter took the stamps and gave them to the boy. And Mr. Crocker took the coins.

"It was just that — " Mr. Crocker said, and smiled.

The man in the apron cleared his throat: — "You never were a father," the man said, "you never knew the feeling of a father, or understood the feeling of a child; and that is why you acted as you did. But a judgement is upon you. God has cursed you. He has afflicted you. He has made you lame and childless as you are — and lame and childless, miserable as you are, you will go to your grave and be forgotten."

And Crocker's wife kept kneading her bony little hands and said, imploringly, "Oh, no — oh don't say that, please don't say that."

The stonecutter, the breath still hoarse in him, left the store. Light came again into the day.

"Well, son," he said, and laid his hand on the boy's back, and "Well, son," he said, "now don't you mind."

They walked across the square, the sheeted spray of iridescent light swept out on them, the horse swizzled at the water-trough, and "Well, son," the stonecutter said.

And the old horse sloped down — ringing with his hoofs upon the cobblestones.

"Well, son," said the stonecutter once again, "be a good boy."

And he trod his own steps then with his great stride and went back again into his shop.

The lost boy stood upon the square, hard by the porches of his father's shop.

"This is Time," thought Grover, "This is Grover, this is Time — "

A car curved out into the square, upon the bill-board of the car-end was a poster and it said St. Louis and Excursion and The Fair.

And light came and went into the Square, and Grover stood there thinking quietly: "Here the Square and here is Grover, here is my father's shop, and here am I."

: *Part* II :

. . . . As we went down through Indiana — you were too
young, child, to remember it — I always think of Grover as
he looked that morning, when we went down through Indiana, going to the Fair. All of the apple trees were coming
out and it was April; all of the trees were coming out. It was
the beginning of the spring in Indiana and everything was

getting green. Of course we don't have farms at home like those in Indiana. Up in the hills, we can't have farms like those. Grover, of course, had never seen such farms as those, and I reckon, boy-like, he had to take it in.

So he sat there with his nose pressed to the window, looking out — I'll never forget him as he sat there looking out the window — he never moved. He looked so earnest, looking out the window — he'd never seen such farms as those, and he was taking it all in. All through that morning we were going down along beside the Wabash River — the Wabash River flows through Indiana, it is the river that they wrote the song about — so all that morning we were going down along the river. And I sat with all you childern gathered about me as we went down through Indiana, going to St. Louis, to the Fair.

The rest of you kept running up and down the aisle — well, no, that's so, you were too young; you were just three, so I kept you with me. But the rest of them kept running up and down the aisle and from one window to another. They kept crossing over from one side to another. They kept calling out and hollering to each other every time they saw something new. They kept trying to look out on all sides and in every way at once, as if they wished they had eyes at the back of their heads. — You see, child, it was the first time any of them had ever been in Indiana, and I reckon that, kid-like, it all seemed strange and new.

And so it seemed like they never could get enough of it. It seemed like they never could be still. They kept running up and down and back and forth, and hollering and shouting to each other, until, "I'll vow! You childern! — I never saw the beat of you!" I said. "The way that you keep running up and down and back and forth and never can be quiet for a minute beats all I ever saw," I said. "I don't see how you keep it up," I said.

You see, I reckon they were all excited about going to St. Louis and so curious over everything they saw. They were so young, and everything seemed so strange and new to them. They couldn't help it, and they wanted to see everything. But — "I'll vow!" I said, "If you childern don't sit down and rest you'll be worn to a frazzle before we ever get to see St. Louis and the Fair!"

Except for Grover! He — no, sir! — not him. Now, boy, I want to tell you — I've raised the lot of you — I've watched you all grow up and go away — and all of you were bright enough, if I do say so, there wasn't a numbskull in the lot. — Why yes! I always said that you were smart enough. — They come around and brag to me today about how smart you are, and I reckon, how you have got on in the world and, as the saying goes, are known about and have a kind of name. — I don't let on, you know. I just sit there and let them talk.

I don't brag on you — if they want to brag on you, that's *their* business. I never bragged on one of my own childern in my life. When father raised us up, we were all brought up that it was not good breedin' to brag about your kin. "If the others want to do it," father said, "well, let *them* do it. Don't ever let on by a word or sign that you know what they are talking about. Just let *them* do the talking, and say nothing."

So when they come around and tell me all about the things you've done — I don't let on to them, I never say a word. — Why yes! — why, here, you know — oh, 'long about a month or so ago, this feller comes — a well-dressed man, you know — he looked intelligent, a good substantial sort of person. — He said he came from New Jersey, or somewhere up in that part of the country — and he began to ask me all sorts of questions, what you were like when you were a boy and all such stuff as that.

I just pretended to study it all over and then I said, "Well, yes" — real serious-like, you know — "well, yes — I reckon I ought to know a little something about him — he was my child, just the same as all the others were — I brought him up just the way I brought up all the others — and" I says — oh, just as solemn as you please, you know — "He wasn't a bad sort of a boy. Why," I says, "up to the time that he was twelve years old he was just about the same as any other boy — a good average normal sort of fellow."

— "Oh," he says — "But didn't you notice something? Wasn't there something kind of strange?" he says, "something different from what you noticed in the other childern?" I didn't let on, you know — I just took it all in and looked as solemn as an owl — I just pretended to study it all over, just as serious as you please. "Why no," I says, real slow-like, after I'd studied it all over, "he had two good eyes and a nose and a mouth, two arms and legs and a good head of hair, and the regular number of fingers and toes just like all the rest of them – now I think if he'd been different from any of the rest of them in those respects I'd have noticed it right off. But as I remember it, he was a good, ordinary, normal sort of boy, just like all the others – " "Yes," he says – oh, all excited-like, you know – "but wasn't he brilliant – didn't you notice how brilliant he was – he must have been more brilliant than the rest!" "Well, now," I says, and pretended to study that all over too. "Now let me see. – Yes," I says. I just looked him in the eye, as solemn as you please – "He did pretty well. He always got promoted. I never heard of the teacher putting a dunce cap on him. But then," I says – "that never happened to any of my other childern either. Now I don't mean to brag on them. I don't believe in bragging on my own kind. If other people want to brag on them, that's their affair; we were just ordinary people, we never pretended to be any different. But I will say *this* much for them – they all had a good fair share of sense and of intelligence. There might not have been any geniuses among them, but they all had their wits about them and I never heard nobody suggest that any of them ought to go to a home for the feebleminded. Now," I says, and I looked him in the eye, you know – "that may not be much, but that's more than I can say of some folks I know. Well," I says, " – well, yes," I says, "I guess he was a fairly bright sort of a boy. I never had no complaints to make of him on that score. He was bright enough," I says, "the only trouble with him — I told him so myself a hundred times, so I'm not telling you anything he hasn't heard before — the only trouble with him," I says, "was, he was lazy."

"Lazy!" he says — oh, you should have seen the look upon his face, you know — he jumped like some one had stuck a pin in him. "Lazy!" he says. "Why, you don't mean to tell me — "

"Yes," I says — oh, I never cracked a smile — "I was telling him the same thing myself the last time that I saw him. I told him it was a mighty lucky thing for him that he had the gift of gab. Of course, he went off to college and read a lot of books, and I reckon that's where he got this flow of language they say he has. . . . But as I said to him the last time that I saw him 'Now look a-here' I said 'If you can earn your living doing a light easy class of work like this you do,' I says, 'you're mighty lucky, because none of the rest of your people,' I says, 'had any such luck as that. They had to work hard for a living.'"

Oh, I told him, you know. I came right out with it. I made no bones about it. And I tell you what — I wish you could have seen his face. It was a study.

"Well," he says, at last, "you've got to admit this, haven't you — he was the brightest boy you had, now wasn't he?"

I just looked at him a moment. I had to tell the truth. I couldn't fool him any longer. "No," I says. "He was a good, bright boy — I've got no complaint to make about him on that score — but the brightest boy I had, the one that surpassed all the rest of them in sense, and understanding, and in judgement — the best boy that I had — the smartest boy I ever saw — was one you never knew — was one you never saw — the boy that was lost."

He looked at me a moment and then he said, "Which boy was that?"

And I tried to tell him. But when I tried to say the word *St. Louis*, I could not. Child, child, the name of that accursed place came back to me — and it was just the same as it had always been. I couldn't say it. I couldn't bear to hear it said. For thirty years or more, whenever any one would say that name to me, or when I heard it anywhere, the thought of it would all come back. And it was like an old raw sore had opened up again — I couldn't help it, it will never change. Child, child, — and when I thought of it again, and when I tried to tell the man, it all came back. I couldn't say it. I had to turn my head away. And I reckon that I cried.

For whenever that old name comes back, I always see him setting there, so earnest-like, with his nose pressed to the window, as we went down through Indiana in the morning, to the Fair. The apple trees were out in bloom, the peach trees too, were out in bloom. All of the trees there are, and everything, were coming out in bloom in April, as we went down along the river, going to the Fair.

And Grover sat there, so still and earnest-like — the other childern were excited, running up and down, shouting to each other, up and down the car — but Grover sat there, looking out the window, and he didn't move. He sat there like a man. He was just eleven and a half years old. Child, child — he was a fine boy, like the paper said [when he died], he had the judgement of one twice his years — he had more

: 39 :

sense, more judgement, and more understanding, than any child I ever saw.

And here, now! — this very morning while he sat there by this gentleman looking out the window — why, yes, this very thing I'm going to tell you proved it — the sense and judgement that he had. — Here we were, you know, going down along the Wabash. We had crossed over into Indiana and, of course, they had no Jim Crow there — and the door opened and here he comes, you know, carrying his valise and swaggering right down the middle of the aisle, as if he owned the place. — Why, Simpson Featherstone, that big old yellow, pock-marked darky which your father got to help us in St. Louis — oh, walks right in, and just as impudent and brazen as you please and starts taking off his overcoat and puts his valise up on the baggage rack, and then sits down and makes himself at home, if you please, as if he owned the railroad. Of course, that's so, we *were* in Indiana and they don't have any law there against the colored people travellin' on the same car with white. So, nigger-like, when we crossed over into Indiana he starts right back out of the nigger car into our own — well, the impudence of him! "Hm," I thought, "now if he thinks he's going to do anything like that, I'll fix him! He'll find out pretty soon who's boss!" So I called out to him, I didn't let on that I knew what he was up to, I just said to him, as serious as a judge, "Simpson," I said, "I guess you made a mistake." "No ma'am," he says, — oh, grinning from ear to ear — "I ain't made no mistake, Miss Eliza." "Oh yes, you have," I said. "Now just take a look around you and see where you are. Now," — I looked him right in the eye — "you get right up and take your suitcase and march right back up that aisle into your own car, where you belong." "Oh no, ma'am," he says, grinning with all his teeth, "I don't have to go back there no more," he says; — "we's in Indiana now, and I can ride anywhere I please."

Then Grover got up and walked right back and looked him in the eye. "No you can't," he said. "Why, what's the reason that I can't?" said Simpson Featherstone. He looked at Grover, sort of startled-like. "Why, Mr. Grover, it's the law," he said. And Grover looked at him and said, "It may be their law, but it's not ours. It's not our way of doing, and it's not your way of doing either. No, you know better," Grover said, "cause you were brought up different. Now you get up and go back where you belong, like mama tells you."

You should have seen the expression on that darky's face. I had to laugh when I thought about it later. Of course, like every one, he respected Grover's judgement — he knew that Grover was right — and he got up, sir, he got right up, sir, without another word. He took his valise and overcoat and marched right up the aisle and out the door to his own car, where he belonged. And that gentleman sitting there beside Grover just turned his head and looked at me and nodded. "I tell you what," he said, "that is certainly a remarkable boy." — Of course, he saw, you know — he understood. He could see that Grover had more sense and character than most grown-ups. And he was right.

So here he was, you know, Grover, this morning, looking out the window at the river, and at all the farms we saw. Because, I reckon, he had never seen such farms as those — and I remember still the way he looked as he sat looking out the window, with his black hair, his eyes as black as tar, and the birthmark on his neck — you and he were the only dark ones that I had, the others were all light and fair and gray-eyed, like their father. But you and he had the Pentland look, when they are dark, the dark Alexander and the Pentland look. You are the spitting image of your uncle Lee, but Grover was the darker of the two.

And so he sat there beside this gentleman, and looked out the window. And then he turned and asked this gentleman every sort of question — what the trees were, what was growing there, how big the farms were — all sorts of questions, which this gentleman would answer, until I said, "Why, I'll vow, Grover! You shouldn't ask so many questions. You'll bother the very life out of this gentleman." — I was afraid, you know, he might annoy this gentleman by asking him so many questions.

The gentleman threw his head back and laughed as big as you please. — I don't know who he was, I never knew his name, but he was a fine-looking man and he had taken a great liking to Grover. — So he threw his head back and laughed and said, "Now you leave that boy alone. He's all right," he said. "He doesn't bother me a bit, and if I know the answers to his questions I will answer him. And if I don't know, I will tell him so. This boy's all right," he said, and put his arm round Grover's shoulders. "So you leave him alone. He doesn't bother me a bit."

And I can still remember how he looked, with his black eyes, his black hair, and with the birthmark on his neck — so grave, so serious, so earnest-like — as he looked out the window at the apple trees, the farms, the barns, the houses and the orchards, taking it all in because it was, I reckon, strange and new to him.

Child, child, it was so long ago, but when I hear the name again, it all comes back, as if it happened yesterday. And the old raw sore is open. I can see him just the way he was, the way he looked, the morning that we went down through Indiana, by the river, going to the Fair.

: *Part* III :

. . . . Can you remember how he looked? . . . . I mean the
birthmark, the black eyes, the olive skin. . . . But I guess you
must have been too young. . . . I was looking at that old
photograph the other day. . . . You know the one I mean? –
That picture showing all of us before the house on Wood-
son Street? . . . . *You* weren't there. . . . *You* didn't get in. . . .
You hadn't arrived. . . . You remember how mad you used to

get when we used to tell you that you were only a dish-rag hanging out in Heaven when something happened? . . . . K-K-K-K-K. . . .

. . . . *You* were the baby. . . . That's what you get for being the baby. . . . You don't get in the picture, do you? . . . . K-K-K-K-K-K. . . . I was looking at that old picture just the other day. . . . There we were. . . . And my God, what is it all about? . . . . Do you ever get to feeling funny? You know what I mean — do you ever get to feeling *queer*? Or do you think about these things? . . . . I mean, does your mind ever go br-r-r- you know what I mean — when you try to figure these things out. . . . Now do you? . . . . Now, I'd like to know. . . . You've been to college and you ought to know the answer. . . . Now did you ever think it over? . . . . Because I'd like to know — you know what I mean? . . . . I wish you'd tell me if you know. . . .

. . . . K-K-K-K-K

. . . . I know, but . . . My God, when I think sometimes of the way I used to be. . . . Now did you ever stop to think that over? . . . . Now I want to ask you. . . . The way you used to be, the way you used to look. . . . Now I'd like to know. . . . I think sometimes of all the dreams I used to have. . . . Playing the piano, practicing seven hours a day, thinking some day I would be a great pianist. . . . Taking singing lessons from Aunt Nell because I felt that some day I was going to have a great career in Opera. . . . K-K-K-K-K. . . . Can you beat it now? . . . . Can you imagine it? . . . . K-K-K-K-K. . . . *Me!* In grand opera! . . . . K-K-K-K-K. . . . Now I want to ask you. . . . I'd like to know. . . .

. . . . Now can you make it out? . . . . Do you know the answer? . . . . Because if you do, I wish you'd tell me. . . . My lord! when I go uptown and walk down the street and look at all these funny-looking little boys and girls hanging around the drug store. . . . It makes me wonder. . . . I mean, their funny little faces. . . . and this funny little talk they have. . . . Do you suppose that *we* were like that. . . . I mean, these funny, awful-looking little things. . . . Do you suppose that was the way we were? . . . . With their cute talk, you know . . . Is that the word for it? . . . . You know what I mean? *Cute* stuff. . . . It makes you wonder. . . . Do you suppose they think of anything except hanging around the drug store and talking cute stuff. . . . Now I'd like to know. . . . Do you suppose any of them have ambitions the way we did? . . . . Do you suppose any of these funny-looking little girls are thinking about a big career in opera? . . . . Didn't you ever see that picture of us — you weren't born I guess when it was made . . . But I was looking at it the other day. . . . It was made before the old house down on Woodson Street, with papa standing in his swallow-tail, and mama there beside him. . . . and Grover, and Ben, and Steve, and Daisy and myself, with our feet upon our bicycles. . . . Luke, poor kid, was only four or five. *He* didn't have a bicycle like us. K-K-K-K-K. . . . But there he was. And there were all of us together and. . . .

Well, there I was, and my poor old skinny legs, and long white dress, and two pigtails hanging down my back. And all the funny-looking clothes we wore, with the doo-lolley business on them, and Ollie Gant was there beside mama and papa, in his Spanish-American War uniform. . . . It was just about that time, can't you remember Ollie in his uniform? . . . . No, of course, you can't. You weren't born.

. . . . But, well, we were a right nice-looking set of people, if I do say so. And there was 86 the way it used to be, with the front porch, and grape vines, and the flower beds before the house. . . . and Miss Eliza standing there by papa, with a watch charm pinned upon her waist. . . . K-K-K-K-K. . . . Do you remember mama and her watch charm. . . . And Miss Amy Partridge, and the Ladies of the Maccabees. . . . K-K-K-K-K. . . . I shouldn't laugh, but Miss Eliza. . . . Well, mama was a pretty woman then. . . . Do you know what I mean? Miss Eliza was a right good-looking woman, and papa there beside her in his swallow-tail. Do you remember how he used to get dressed up on Sunday? . . . . And how grand we thought he was. . . . And how he let me take his money out and count it. . . . And how rich we all thought he was. . . . And how wonderful that little dinkey marble shop on the square looked to us. . . . K-K-K-K-K. . . . Can you beat it Now? . . . . Why we thought that papa was the biggest man in town and. . . . Oh, you can't tell me! You can't tell me! He had his faults, but papa was a wonderful man. You know he was!

. . . . And there was Ben and Grover, Daisy, Luke and me. . . . All of us lined up there before the house with one foot on our bicycles. . . . And I got to thinking back about it all. It all came back.

. . . . He was a sweet kid. Can you remember him at all? Do you remember anything about him? The way he looked there in St. Louis. . . . You were only three or four years old then, but you must remember something . . . Do you remember how you used to bawl when I would scrub you? . . . . K-K-K-K-K. . . . Do you remember that? . . . . Don't you remember how I'd get you in the tub and scrape all the hide off of you. . . . And how you'd bawl for Grover? . . . . K-K-K-K-K. . . . Poor kid, you used to yell for Grover every time I'd get you in the tub. . . . K-K-K-K-K. . . .

I was a little slavey around mama's house. . . . and so used to scrubbing floors that I guess I treated you just like I treated one of mama's rooms when I got you in the tub. . . . K-K-K-K-K. . . . Have you forgotten now? . . . . Can't you remember it? . . . .

I hadn't thought of it for years until the other day, and then I came across that picture, and it all came back to me . . . Grover was working at the Inside Inn out on the Fair Grounds. . . .

. . . . Do you remember the old Inside Inn? . . . . That big old wooden thing inside the Fair? . . . . And how I used to take you there to wait for Grover when he got through working? . . . . and old fat Billy Pelham at the newsstand. . . . how he always used to give you a stick of chewing gum? . . . . K-K-K-K-K. . . . Do you remember Billy Pelham and his chewing gum? . . . .

They were all crazy about Grover. . . . Everybody liked him. . . . He was a sweet kid. . . . And how proud Grover was of you? . . . . How he used to show you off? . . . . . How he used to take you around and make you talk to Billy Pelham? . . . . And Mr. Curtis at the desk? . . . . And that bellboy they called Prince Albert? . . . . . . Poor old gawky Albert Fox. . . . K-K-K-K-K. . . . Don't you remember Albert Fox? . . . . .

And how Grover would try to make you talk and get you to say 'Grover'? . . . . And you couldn't say it? . . . . . You couldn't pronounce the 'r'? . . . . And you'd say 'Gwovah.' . . . . . Have you forgotten that? . . . . . You shouldn't forget *that*, because. . . . you were a *cute* kid, then. . . . Ho-ho-ho-ho-ho. . . . You know what I mean? . . . . I don't know where it's gone to, but you were a big hit in those days. . . . K-K-K-K-K. You oughtn't to forget that. Because, I tell you, boy, you were Somebody back in those days. . . .

. . . . I was thinking of it all the other day when I was looking at that photograph. . . . How we used to go and meet him there and how he'd take us to the Midway. . . . Do you remember the Midway? . . . . The Snake-Eater, and the Living Skeleton, the Fat Woman and the Shoot the Chute, the Scenic Railway and the Ferris Wheel? . . . . . How you bawled the night we took you on the Ferris Wheel? . . . . You yelled your head off. . . . I tried to laugh it off, but I tell you, I was scared myself. . . . Back in those days, that was Something. . . . And how Grover laughed at us and told us there was no danger. . . . My Lord! poor little Grover. He was only twelve years old, and how grown up he seemed to us . . . I was two years older, but I thought he knew it all. . . .

Poor kid, he always brought us something — some ice cream or some candy, something he had bought out of the poor little money he'd gotten at the Fair. . . .

. . . . So we had come downtown one afternoon. . . . I guess we both had sneaked away from home. . . . Mama had gone out somewhere. . . . And Grover and I got on the street car and came downtown. . . . And my lord, we thought that we were going somewhere. . . . In those days, that was what we called a *trip*. . . . A ride in the street car was something to write home about in those days. . . . I hear that it's all built up around there now. . . .

So we got on the car there at the King's Highway and rode the whole way down into the business section of St. Louis. . . . We got out on Washington Street and walked up and down. . . . And I tell you, boy, we thought that that was something. Grover took me into a drug store and set me up to soda water. Then we came out and walked around some more, down to the Union Station and clear over to the river. . . . And both of us half scared to death at what we'd done and wondering what mama would say if she found out.

. . . . We stayed down there till it was getting dark, and we went by a lunch room. . . . an old one-armed joint with one-armed chairs and people sitting on stools and eating at the counter. . . . We read all the signs to see what they had to eat and how much it cost, and I guess nothing on the menu was more than fifteen cents, but it couldn't have looked grander to us if it had been Delmonico's. . . . So we stood there with our noses pressed against the window, looking in . . . Two skinny little kids, both of us scared half to death, getting the thrill of a lifetime out of it. . . . You know what I mean? . . . . And smelling everything with all our might and thinking how good it all smelled. . . . Then Grover turned to me and whispered, "Come on, Helen. . . . Let's go in. . . . It says fifteen cents for pork and beans. . . . And I've got the money," Grover said. . . . "I've got sixty cents."

. . . . I was so scared I couldn't speak. . . . I'd never been in a place like that before. . . . But I kept thinking, "Oh lord, if mama should find out.". . . . I felt as if we were committing some big crime. . . . Don't you know what I mean? Don't you know how it is when you're a kid? It was the thrill of a lifetime . . . I couldn't resist. So we both went in and sat down on those high stools before the counter and ordered pork and beans and a cup of coffee. . . . I suppose we were too frightened at what we'd done really to enjoy anything. We just gobbled it all up in a hurry, and gulped our coffee down. And I don't know whether it was the excitement. . . . I guess the poor kid was already sick and didn't know it. But I turned and looked at him and he was white as death. . . . And when I asked him what was the matter he wouldn't tell me. . . . He was too proud. He said he was all right, but I could see that he was sick as a dog. . . . So he paid the bill. . . . It came to forty cents, I'll never forget *that* as long as I live. . . . And sure enough, we no more got out the door — he'd scarcely time to reach the curb — before it all came up. . . .

And the poor kid was so scared and so ashamed. And what scared him so was not that he had gotten sick but that he had spent all that money, and it had come to nothing. And mama would find out. . . . Poor kid, he just stood there looking at me and he whispered, "Oh Helen, don't tell mama. She'll be mad when she finds out." Then we hurried home, and he was burning up with fever when we got there.

. . . . Mama was waiting for us. . . . — She looked at us, you know how Miss Eliza looks at you, when she thinks you've been doing something that you shouldn't? . . . . Mama said, "Why, where on earth have you two children been?" — I guess she was all set to lay us out. Then she took one look at Grover's face. That was enough for her. . . . She said: "Why, child, what in the world!" — She was white as a sheet herself. . . . And all that Grover said was "Mama, I feel sick.". . . .

. . . . And he fell over on the bed, and we undressed him and mama put her hand upon his forehead and came out in the hall — she was so white you could have made a black mark on her face with chalk — and whispered to me, "Go get the doctor quick, he's burning up."

And I went chasing up the street, my pigtails flying, to Dr. Packer's house. I brought him back with me. When he came out of Grover's room I heard him tell her. "Typhoid fever.". . . . And I think she knew it then. . . . I think she knew it. . . . He'd had it once before. She never gave up till the end. . . . She never let us know that she had given up. . . . But she knew it then. She knew it.

. . . . I looked at her. Her face was white as a sheet. She looked at me and looked right through me. . . . She never saw me. And I heard her say, "Gone. . . . Gone". . . . Just like that. And oh, my God, I'll never forget the way she looked, the way she said it, the way my heart stopped and came up in my throat. . . . And poor mama. . . . I was only a little slavey kid in that old rooming house. I was a skinny little kid of fourteen. But I knew that she was dying right before my eyes. . . . I knew that I was looking on at death right there. I knew that if she lived to be a hundred she'd never get over it, never be able to forget about it, that it would be like death every time she thought about it.

. . . . Poor old mama. You know, she never got over it. He was her eyeballs, she thought more of him than she did of any of the others and. . . . poor little Grover! . . . . He was a sweet kid, I can still see him lying there white as a sheet and during all those weeks that followed, how he lay there till he wasted away to a little bundle of skin and bones.

. . . . It all came back to me the other day when I was looking at that picture, and I thought, my God, we were two kids together, and I was only two years older than Grover was. . . . And now I'm forty-six, and Grover would be forty-four if he had lived. . . . Can you believe it? Can you imagine that? . . . . My lord, he seemed so grown-up to me. He was such a quiet kind of kid. . . . Do you know what I mean? He was only a kid, yet he seemed older than the rest of us.

. . . . And when I think of those two funny little kids with their noses pressed against the window of that old cheap lunch room. . . . And how natural it all seemed, how thrilling and how wonderful. . . . And how scared we were that mama would find out. . . . And how we hurried home, and how white he was, and how long ago all that has been. . . . And then I see a picture and it all comes back – the boarding house, St. Louis, and the Fair. . . . And all of it just the same as it has always been, as if it happened yesterday. . . . And all of us have grown up, and I am forty-six years old. And nothing has turned out the way I thought it would. . . . And all my hopes and dreams and big ambitions have all come to nothing. . . .

Then it all comes back again, two frightened, funny little kids, alone, way out there in St. Louis, their noses glued against the window of a cheap lunch room. . . . and Grover with the birthmark on his neck. . . . Can you remember anything of how he looked? The way it was – the house we lived in? . . . . The night he died and how I came and got you, picked you up and took you in to look at him. . . . That old house that we lived in, on the corner. . . . The pantry and the way it smelled. . . . The roomers, St. Louis, and the Fair. . . .

It's all so long ago, as if it happened in another world. And then it all comes back, as if it happened yesterday. . . . And sometimes I will lie awake at night and think of all the people who have come and gone and all the things that happened. And how everything is different from the way we thought that it would be. And hear the trains down by the river, and the whistles and the bell. . . . And how we went to St. Louis back in 1904. . . .

And then I go out on the street and see the faces of the people that I pass. . . . Don't they look strange to you? Don't you see something funny in their eyes, as if they all were puzzled about something? . . . . Now am I crazy, or do you know what I mean? . . . . Now you've been to college and I want to know. . . . I want you to tell me if you know the answer. . . . I mean that funny look they have, that queer look in the eyes. . . . Now do you know what I mean? . . . . Do they look that way to you? . . . . Did you ever notice it when you were a kid? . . . .

My God, I wish I knew the answer to these things. . . . I'd like to find out what is wrong. . . . What has changed since then. . . . . And if we look that way to them. . . . And if we too have changed. . . . And if we have that same queer funny look in our eyes too. . . . And if it happens to us all, to every one. . . .

. . . . The way it all turns out is nothing like the way we thought that it would be. . . . And how it all gets lost, until it seems that it has never happened. . . . that it is something that we dreamed somewhere. . . . You see what I mean now? . . . . That it is something that we heard somewhere, that it happened to some one else. . . . And then it all comes back again.

. . . . And there you are, two funny, frightened skinny little kids with their noses pressed against a dirty window thirty years ago. . . . The way it felt, the way it smelled, even the funny smell in that old pantry of our house. And the steps before the house, the way the rooms looked. Those two little boys in sailor suits who used to ride up and down before the house on their tricycles. . . . And the birthmark on his neck. . . . The Inside Inn. . . . St. Louis, and the Fair. . . . It all comes back as if it happened yesterday. And then it goes away and seems farther off and stranger than if it happened in a dream. . . .

Part IV

. . . . "*This* is King's Highway," a man said.

And then I looked and saw that it was just a street. There were some big new buildings, a big hotel, some restaurants and "bar-grill" places, of the modern kind, the livid monotone of Neon lights, the ceaseless traffic of the motor cars — all this was new, but it was just a street. And I knew that it had always been a street, and nothing more — but somehow — I stood there looking at it, wondering what else I had expected to find.

The man kept looking at me with inquiry, and I asked him if the Fair had not been out this way.

"Sure, the Fair was out beyond here," the man said. "Where the park is now. But this street you're looking for? — Don't you remember the name of the street or nothin'?" the man said.

I said I thought the name of the street was Edgemont Street, but that I was not sure. But that it was something like that. And I said the house was on the corner of this street and of another street. And then the man said, "What street was that?" I said I did not know but that the house was on the corner of the street, and that King's Highway was a block or so away and that an interurban line ran past about half a block or so from where we lived.

"What line was this?" the man said, and stared at me.

"The interurban line," I said.

Then he stared at me again and at the man with him, and finally, "I don't know no interurban line," he said.

I said it was a line that ran behind some houses and that there were board fences there and grass beside the tracks. I said it seemed to go right through somewhere behind some houses. But somehow I could not say that it was summer in those days and that you could smell the ties, a kind of wooden tarry smell, and feel a kind of absence in the afternoon after the car had gone. I only said the interurban line was back behind somewhere between the back yards of some houses and some old board fences, and that King's Highway was a block or two away.

I did not say King's Highway had not been a street in those days but a kind of road that wound from magic out of some dim and haunted land and that along the way it had got mixed in with Tom the Piper's son, with hot cross buns, with all the light that came and went, and with cloud shadows passing on the mountains, with coming down through Indiana in the morning, and the smell of engine smoke, the Union Station, and most of all with voices lost and far and long ago that said "King's Highway."

I didn't say these things about King's Highway because I looked about me, and I saw what King's Highway was. King's Highway was a street, a broad and busy street with new hotels and hard bright lights, and endless flocks of motors swarming up and down. All I could say was that the street was near King's Highway, and was on the corner, and that the interurban trolley line was close to there. I said it was a stone house, and that there were stone steps before it, and a strip of grass. I said I thought the house had had a turret at one corner, I could not be sure.

The men looked at me again, and one said, "This is King's Highway, but we never heard of any street like that."

I left them then and went on till I found the place. And again, again, I turned into the street, finding the place where the two corners meet, the huddled block, the turret, and the steps, and paused a moment, looking back, as if the street was Time.

So I waited for a moment for a word, and for a door to

open, for the child to come. I waited, but no words were spoken; no one came.

Yet all of it was just as it had always been except the steps were lower and the porch less high, the strip of grass less wide than I had thought, but all the rest of it as I had known it would be. A graystone front, three-storied, with a slant slate roof, the side red brick and windowed, still with the old arched entrance in the center for the doctor's use.

There was a tree in front, a lamp post, and behind and to the side more trees than I had known there would be. And all the slatey turret gables, all the slatey window gables going into points, the two arched windows, in strong stone, in the front room. The small stone porch, stone-carved, with its roof of gabled slate beside.

And it was all so strong, so solid and so ugly – and all, save for the steps and grass, so enduring and so good, the way I had remembered it, the way I knew that I would not get fooled, the way I knew it would not lie to me, really just the way that it had always been, except I did not smell the tar, the hot and caulky dryness of the old cracked ties, the boards of backyard fences and the coarse and sultry grass, and absence in the afternoon when the street car had gone, and the twins, sharp-visaged in their sailor suits, pumping with furious shrillness on tricycles up and down before the house, and Simpson coming back from somewhere with his basket, and the feel of the hot afternoon, and that every one was absent at the Fair.

Except for this, it all was just the same, except for this and for King's Highway, which was now a street, except for this, King's Highway, and the child that did not come.

It was a hot day. Darkness had come, the heat rose up and hung and sweltered like a sodden blanket in St. Louis. It was wet heat, and one knew that there would be no relief or coolness in the night, and one knew the heat would stay. And when one tried to think of the time when the heat would go away, one said, "It cannot last. It's bound to go away," as we always say it in America. But one did not believe it when he said it. The heat soaked down and men sweltered in it, the faces of the people were pale and greasy with the heat. And in their faces was a kind of patient wretchedness, and one felt the kind of desolation that one feels at the end of a hot day in a great city in America — when one's home is far away, across the continent, and he thinks of all that distance, all that heat, and feels, "Oh God! but it's a big country!"

The way it made one feel was the way one feels when he is far away and all alone in a big city on a day like this, and hears the sound of trains, of bells, of engine whistles, and of boats out on the river, and when he walks along the street beneath hot clusters of electric light, or seeks the park — the bleached grass, the littered rubbish of soiled newspapers, and people sprawled out on the yellowed grass — or when he sees the kind of bench they put in the parks here in America to make one cheerful at the end of a hot day — a concrete bench, with the hard hot glare of dead electric light upon it, so that people will behave themselves, and with a concrete arm or barrier across the middle, so that people won't lie down.

Or it makes one feel the way one feels in a city like this when he comes out on an open place, a fine square, a civic center, and sees a fine new city hall or community center, all lighted up with searchlights and surrounded by fine new standard lamp posts, each with five hard grapes of dead electric light. He sees men in shirtsleeves and sag faces lounging at the corners, or women sitting on the porches with no stockings on, relapsing limply to the heat with the hard hot white of dead electric light upon them.

And he hears the trains, the engine whistles and the boats out on the river, and thinks of all that distance, all that heat, and not with joy, and not with hope, and not as one who thinks of the Great West and of the rampart of the shining mountains, but as some one drowned and lost and sunken on the sea floors of unending desolation, as of some one swimming in a dream.

He knows that it is endless, he is drowned, that he cannot escape. He knows that he is lost and sunken in America, that it is too big for him, and that he has no home. He knows he cannot grasp and hold it or comprise it, shape it to a flaming word, as once, in the exultant hope and madness of youth and loneliness and night, he *knew* he could. He knows now that he is only a nameless atom lost in vacancy, a brief and dusty cipher, whirled homelessly in unnumbered time, and that all the dreams, the strength, the passion, the belief of youth have gone amort.

And he feels nothing but absence, absence, and the desolation of America, the loneliness and sadness of the high, hot skies, and evening coming on across the Middle West, across the sweltering and heat-sunken land, across all the lonely little towns, the farms, the fields, the oven swelter of Ohio, Kansas, Iowa and Indiana at the close of day, and voices, casual in heat, voices at the little stations, quiet, casual, somehow faded into that enormous vacancy and weariness of heat, of space, and of the immense, the sorrowful and most high and awful skies.

Then he hears the engine and the wheel again, the wailing whistle and the bell, the sound of shifting in the sweltering yard, and walks the street, and walks the street, beneath the clusters of hard lights, and by the people with sagged faces, and is drowned in desolation and in no belief. "Why here? What shall I do now? Where shall I go?"

He feels the way one feels when one comes back, and knows that he should not have come, and when he sees that, after all, King's Highway is – a street; and St. Louis – the enchanted name – a big hot common town upon the river, sweltering in wet dreary heat, and not quite South, and nothing else enough to make it better.

It had not been like this before. I could remember how it would get hot, and how good the heat was, and how I would lie out in the back yard on an airing mattress, and how the mattress would get hot and dry and smell like a hot mattress full of sun, and how the sun would make me want to sleep, and how, sometimes, I would go down into the basement to feel coolness, and how the cellar smelled as cellars always smell – a kind of cool, stale smell, a smell of cobwebs and of grimy bottles. And I would remember, when you opened the door upstairs, and went down to the cellar, the smell of the cellar would come up to you – cool, musty, stale and dank and dark – and how the thought of the dark cellar always filled me with a kind of numb excitement, a kind of visceral expectancy.

I could remember how it got hot in the afternoons, and how I would feel absence in the afternoons, a sense of absence and vague sadness in the afternoons, when every one had gone away. The house would seem so lonely in the afternoons, and sometimes I would sit inside, on the second step of the hall stairs, and listen to the sound of silence and of absence in the afternoon. I could smell the oil upon the floor and on the stairs, and see the sliding doors with their brown varnish and the beady chains across the door, and thrust my hands among the beady chains, and gather them together in my arms, and let them clash, and swish with light beady swishings all round me. I could feel darkness, absence, varnished darkness and stained light, within the house, through the stained glass of the window on the stairs, through the small stained glasses by the door, stained light and absence, silence and the smell of floor oil and vague sadness in the house in a hot mid-afternoon. And all these things themselves would have a kind of life: would seem to wait attentively, to be most living and most still.

I would sit there and listen. I could hear the girl next door practice her piano lessons in the afternoon, and hear the street car coming by between the backyard fences, half a block away, and smell the dry and sultry smell of backyard fences, the smell of coarse hot grasses by the car track in the afternoon, the smell of tar, of dry caulked ties, the smell of bright worn flanges, and feel the loneliness of back yards in the afternoon and the sense of absence, absence, when the car is gone.

Then I would long for evening and return, the slant of light, and feet along the street, the sharp-faced twins in sailor suits upon their tricycles, the smell of supper and the sound of voices in the house again, and Grover coming from the Fair.

. . . . And again, again, I turned into the street, finding the place where the two corners meet, turning at last to see if Time was there. I passed the house, some lights were burning in the house, the door was open and a woman sat upon the porch. And presently I turned and stopped before the house again. The corner light fell blank upon the house. I stood looking at the house a moment, and I put my foot upon the step.

Then I said to the woman who was sitting on the porch: "This house. . . . excuse me. . . . but could you tell me, please, who lives here in this house."

I knew my words were strange and hollow and I had not said what I wished to say. She stared at me a moment, puzzled.

Then she said, "I live here. Who are you looking for?" she said.

I said, "Why, I am looking for. . . ."

And then I stopped, because I knew I could not tell her what it was that I was looking for. My words were wrenched and foolish now when I felt her looking at me, and I did not know what to say.

"There used to be a house — " I said.

The woman was now staring hard at me. I said – "I think I used to live here" – she said nothing.

In a moment I continued – "I used to live here in this house," I said, "when I was a little boy."

She was silent for a moment, looking at me, then she said, "Oh. Are you sure this was the house? Do you remember the address?"

"I have forgotten the address," I said, "but it was Edgemont Street, and it was on the corner. And I know this is the house."

"This isn't Edgemont Street," the woman said, "the name is Bates."

"Well, then, they changed the name of the street," I said, "but this is the same house. It hasn't changed."

She was silent a moment, then she nodded: "Yes. They did change the name of the street. I remember hearing that it used to have another name. When I was a child they called it something else," she said. "But that was a long time ago. When was it that you lived here?"

"In 1904."

Again she was silent, looking at me for a moment. Then presently: "Oh. . . . That was the year of the Fair. You were here then?"

"Yes," I now spoke rapidly, with more confidence, "my mother had the house, and we were here for seven months. . . . and the house belonged to Dr. Packer," – I went on – "We rented it from him – "

"Yes," the woman said, and nodded now – "this was Dr. Packer's house. I never knew him. I've only been here a few years, but Dr. Packer owned this house . . . He's dead now, he's been dead for many years. But this was the Packer house, all right," the woman said.

"That entrance on the side," I said, "where the steps go up, that was for Dr. Packer's patients. That was the entrance to his office. That's the way his patients came and went."

"Oh," the woman said, "I didn't know that. I've often wondered what it was. I didn't know what it was for."

"And this big room in front here," I continued, "that was the doctor's office. And there were sliding doors, and next to it, a kind of alcove for his patients – "

"Yes, the alcove is still there, only all of it has been made into one room now – and I never knew just what the alcove was for."

" – And there were sliding doors on this side too that opened on the hall – and a stairway going up upon this side. And half way up the stairway, at the landing, a little window of colored glass – and across the sliding doors here in the hall, a kind of curtain made of strings of beads."

She nodded, smiling. "Yes, it's just the same – we still have the sliding doors and the stained glass window on the stairs. There's no bead curtain any more," she said, "but I remember when people had them. I know what you mean."

"When we were here," I said, "we used the doctor's office for a parlor – except later on – the last month or two – and then we used it for – a bedroom."

"It is a bedroom now," she said. "I run the house – I rent rooms – all of the rooms upstairs are rented – but I have two brothers and they sleep in this front room."

And we were silent for a moment, then I said, "My brother stayed there too."

"In the front room?" the woman said.

I answered "Yes."

She paused a moment, then she said, "Won't you come in? I don't believe it's changed much. Would you like to see?"

I thanked her and I said I would, and I went up the steps. She opened the screen door and I went into the house.

And it was just the same, – the stairs, the hallway, and the sliding doors, the window of stained glass upon the stairs. And all of it was just the same, except for absence, absence, in the afternoon, the stained light of absence in the afternoon, and the child who sat there, waiting on the stairs, and something fading like a dream, something coming like a light, something going, passing, fading, like the shadows of a wood.

It was all the same except that I had sat there feeling things were *Somewhere* – and now I *knew*. I had sat there feeling that a vast and sultry river was somewhere – and now I knew! I had sat there wondering what King's Highway was, where it began, and where it ended – now I knew! I had sat there haunted by the magic word "downtown" – now I knew! – and by the street car, after it had gone – and by all things that came and went and came again, like the cloud shadows passing in a wood, that never could be captured – the memory of another house, and sunlight, April, and the seasons passing, as the shadows pass, a train, a river, morning and the hills of home.

For all would come again, and I would sit there on the stairs, in absence, absence, in the afternoon, and try to get it back again. And it would come and go and come again until I had it back, I had it back, and it was mine and I could remember all that I had seen and been – that yet had all the lights of time on it, the shadowy echoes of a thousand lives, that brief sum of me, the universe of my four years that was so short to measure, so far, so endless to remember.

It would all come back to me like his dark eyes, his quiet face. And I would see my small face pooled in the dark mirror of the hall, my grave eyes, and my quiet self, the lone integrity of Me, and know that I was just a child, yet know all-clearly that a man could ever know, which was, "Here – a child, my core, my kernel – and here House and here House listening – and here absence, absence in the afternoon – oh utter universe, I know you: – here am I!"

And then it would be gone again, fading like cloud shadows in the hills, going like lost faces in a dream, coming like the vast, the drowsy rumors of the distant and enchanted Fair, and coming, going, coming, being found and lost, possessed and held and never captured, like lost voices in the mountains, long ago, like the dark eyes and the quiet face, the dark lost boy, my brother, who himself like shadows, or like absence in the house, would come, would go, and would return again.

The woman took me back into the house and through the hall. I told her of the pantry, and I told her where it was and pointed to the place, but now it was no longer there. And I told her of the back yard, and the old board fence around the yard. But the old board fence was gone. And I told her of the carriage house, and told her it was painted red. But now there was a small garage. And the back yard was still there, but smaller than I thought, and now there was a tree.

"I did not know there was a tree," I said. "I do not remember any tree."

"Perhaps it was not there," she said, "a tree could grow in thirty years." And then we came back through the house again and paused a moment at the sliding doors.

"And could I see this room?" I said.

She slid the doors back. They slid open smoothly, with a kind of rolling heaviness, as they used to do. And then I saw the room again. It was the same. There was a window to the side, the two arched windows to the front, the alcove and the sliding doors, the fireplace with the tiles of mottled green, the mantel of dark mission wood, the mantel posts, a dresser and a bed, just where the dresser and the bed had been so long ago.

"Is this the room?" the woman said. "It hasn't changed?"

I told her that it was the same.

"And your brother slept here where my brothers sleep?"

"This was his room," I said.

And we were silent for a moment. I turned to go, and I said, "Well, thank you. I appreciate your showing me."

And she said that she was glad and that it was no trouble. And she said, "And when you see your family — you can tell them that you saw the house," she said. "And my name is Mrs. Bell. You can tell your mother that a Mrs. Bell has got the house. And when you see your brother, you can tell him that you saw the room he slept in, and that you found it just the same."

I told her then that he was dead.

The woman was silent for a moment. Then she looked at me and said, "He died here, didn't he? In this room?"

And I told her that he did.

"Well, then," she said, "I knew it. I don't know how. But when you told me he was here, I knew it."

I said nothing. In a moment the woman said: "What did he die of?"

"Typhoid."

She looked shocked and troubled, and said involuntarily: "My two brothers — "

"That was a long time ago," I said. "I don't think you need to worry now."

"Oh. I wasn't thinking about that," she said. — "It was just hearing that a little boy — your brother — was — was in this room that my two brothers sleep in now — "

"Well, maybe I shouldn't have told you, then. But he was a good boy — and if you'd known him you wouldn't mind."

She said nothing, and I added quickly: "Besides, he didn't stay here long. This wasn't really his room — but the night he came back with my sister he was so sick — they didn't move him."

"Oh," the woman said, "I see." And in a moment: "Are you going to tell your mother you were here?"

"I don't think so."

"I — I wonder how she feels about this room."

"I don't know. She never speaks of it."

"Oh . . . . . . How old was he?"

"He was twelve."

"You must have been pretty young yourself."

"I was four."

"And . . . . you just wanted to see the room, didn't you? That's why you came back."

"Yes."

"Well" – indefinitely – "I guess you've seen it now."

"Yes, thank you."

"I guess you don't remember much about him, do you? I shouldn't think you would."

"No, not much."

. . . . The years dropped off like fallen leaves: the face came back again – the soft dark oval, the dark eyes, the soft brown berry on the neck, the raven hair, all bending down, approaching – the whole ghost-wise, intent and instant, like faces from a haunted wood.

"Now say it: *Grover!*"

"Gova."

"No – not Gova: *Grover*. . . . Say it!"

"Gova."

"Ah-h – you *didn't* say it. . . . You said Gova: *Grover* . . . now say it."

"Gova."

"Look, I'll tell you what I'll do if you say it right. . . . Would you like to go down to King's Highway? Would you like Grover to set you up? All right then. . . . . . if you say Grover and say it right, I'll take you to King's Highway and set you up to ice cream. . . . Now say it right: *Grover*."

"Gova."

"Ah-h, you-u. You're the craziest old boy I ever did see: can't you even say Grover?"

"Gova."

"Ah-h you-u. . . . . old tongue-tie, that's what you are. Some day I'm going to. . . . Well, come on, then. I'll set you up anyway. . . . ."

It all came back and faded and was lost again. I turned to go, and thanked the woman and I said: "Good-bye."

"Well, then, good-bye," the woman said, and we shook hands. "I'm glad if I could show you. I'm glad if — " She did not finish, and at length she said, "Well, then, that was a long time ago. You'll find it all changed now, I guess. It's all built up around here now, — way out beyond here, out beyond where the Fair grounds used to be. I guess you'll find it changed," she said.

And we could find no more to say. We stood there for a moment on the steps, and shook hands once more.

"Well, then, good-bye."

And again, again, I turned into the street, finding the place where corners meet, turning to look again to see where Time had gone. And all was there as it had always been. And all was gone, and never would come back again. And all of it was just the same, it seemed that it had never changed since then, except all had been found and caught and captured for forever. And so, finding all, I knew all had been lost.

And I knew that I would never come again, and that lost magic would not come again, — and that the light that came, that passed and went and that returned again, the memory of lost voices in the hill, cloud shadows passing in the mountains, the voices of our kinsman long ago, the street, the heat, King's Highway, and the piper's son, the vast drowsy murmur of the distant Fair, — oh strange and bitter miracle of time — come back again.

But I knew that it could not come back — the cry of absence in the afternoon, the house that waited and the child that dreamed; and through the thicket of man's memory, from the enchanted wood, the dark eye and the quiet face, — poor child, life's stranger and life's exile, lost, like all of us, a cipher in blind mazes, long ago — my parent, friend, and brother, the lost boy, was gone forever and would not return.

E*ditorial* p*olicy*

I have edited this unexpurgated text of *The Lost Boy* in the
Gant cycle, with Grover as the title character. The relevant
typescript I used is in the William B. Wisdom Collection of
Thomas Wolfe Papers, Houghton Library, Harvard University: bMS Am 1883 (1027–1032). In these folders I also found
manuscript copy for a very few of the hundreds of pages of
typescript. Each of the four parts of the novella is represented in two or three stages in this material. It was Wolfe's
habit in early 1937 to dictate most of his fiction. His longhand additions, deletions, refinements, and specific instructions for incorporating his additions are evident throughout
the typescript. Elizabeth Nowell's handwriting is obvious
in word counts, notes, suggested excisions, and occasional
words to clarify Wolfe's text.

In one instance in Part I, I have bracketed two of
Nowell's words. These words also appear in the 1937 *Redbook*
short story drawn from this novella. I have also bracketed
three additional words inserted by his agent in the typescript of Part II. The typescript passage containing these
three words is not included in the 1937 short story. In this
case it is clear from the typescript that the author considered and accepted Nowell's clarification of his meaning.
The most significant of Wolfe's own longhand additions to
the final stage of the typescript for the novella are Mr.
Gant's berating of Mr. Crocker in Part I and several vital
lines of the brother's conversation with Mrs. Bell in Part IV.

I have attempted to maintain the integrity of the work by presenting *The Lost Boy* in a form as close to the original version of the novella as possible. Occasional typographical errors and obvious mistakes in spelling and punctuation I have silently corrected. The most significant of my clarifications is in Part III: I have changed the spelling of "Chute the Chute" to "Shoot the Chute." This correction of the first word is consistent with the 1937 *Redbook* text. Throughout I have used the most frequent spelling of repeated words that are presented inconsistently in the edited typescript. For example, I have used *towards* instead of *toward*. To minimize the distractions for readers, I have also consistently capitalized street addresses, proper names of buildings, historic events, and natural features such as rivers and regions: Woodson Street, Union Station, Spanish-American War, Wabash River, and the North.

By retaining Wolfe's original paragraphing and honoring his stylistic idiosyncrasies, I have striven to preserve the Gantian authenticity of this text. I have reproduced his customary separation of compound words such as *some one* and *any more*. I have followed his hyphenation of words, intruding only for the sake of consistency. Dashes and dots as Wolfe employed them to suggest pauses and personal mannerisms of speech, as well as to function in place of ordinary punctuation marks, are faithfully reproduced in all instances as they appear in the typescript, though I have removed or added the occasional space between an ellipsis and the text preceding it in order to provide some visual consistency. In Part III this complex stylistic practice of the author is very conspicuous in his characterization of Helen and the presentation of her staccato monologue about life and Grover. I have also preserved Wolfe's underscoring (typeset as italic) and capitalization for emphasis. A special instance of capitalization for this purpose is his treatment of the word *square* in Part I. At very significant moments during Grover's afternoon experience, Wolfe capitalized this word; whenever it appears as a mere point of reference, it is a lowercase word in the typescript and in this text. Incidentally, Wolfe presents *mama* and *papa* without capitalization except when either word begins a sentence. At one point he also lets stand, as I do, the apparently ungrammatical statement that Grover "drunk" a "glorious and pervasive smell into his lungs."

I believe *The Lost Boy* in this form will give readers an appreciation of Thomas Wolfe's glorious and pervasive achievement in the novella.